The

My Smile

Alexis Moreira

Alexis Moreira Publishing

ISBN
9780692910696

DEDICATION

This is dedicated to my three children: Ricardo Ayala Jr.;
Samia Boines; and Jason Boines Jr.

CONTENTS

4

1 MY LIFE NOW

I am a thirty-seven-year-old biracial woman with three children. I am living with multiple sclerosis. Multiple sclerosis (MS) is an autoimmune disease that attacks the central nervous system. I was diagnosed with multiple sclerosis on December 8, 2008. While there is currently no cure for multiple sclerosis, to help slow the progression of the disease I take an injection every day—and I will have to every day for the rest of my life. I also require a home attendant for twelve hours a day, seven days a week. Before I was diagnosed with MS I worked as a case manager and a preschool teacher. I was also in my third year in college, studying liberal arts and minoring in sociology. I had a full life. But at this current moment, I even need assistance walking most of the time. My lower extremities are very weak. I can walk—slowly—and my balance is off, so I fall frequently. I need assistance getting dressed, taking a shower, and taking care of my children. There are many reasons why I have to be strong even when I think I can't be. For starters, those reasons are my two boys (ages Twenty and Ten) and my girl (age Twelve). My life, my upbringing, and my experiences being a mother have made me into the strong woman who I am today.

2 MY CHILDHOOD

When I was a child, my mother and father were married. I was the baby of three children—two girls and one boy. My mom stayed home, and my dad worked as an engineer. My mother and father separated when I was six years old due to my father drinking and cheating on my mother.

My father was the provider for the family. When he left, my mother had to turn to government assistant to provide for me and my older siblings. Then she became curious about drugs and started smoking crack. My mother also began dating a new guy—he was nice at first. After a while, she got pregnant with my little sister. She continued to smoke crack during her pregnancy. Things started to get out of control. One day, my aunts came to my school to pick me up early. Someone had called Administration for Children's Services (ACS) on my mother. She would smoke in the house while we were playing in the other room. Eventually, we lost the apartment and had to move in with my grandmother.

My grandmother lived on the sixth floor in her apartment complex. She had a full house. It was me, my mother, my siblings, my cousins, and all of my aunts and uncles living under one roof. My mother was rarely there. She would leave for a couple of days at a time. I knew that was very strange, but I didn't pay it any mind. While staying at my grandmother's house, food was very scarce. There were some nights that my sibling's and cousins and I couldn't eat dinner. My grandmother simply couldn't afford to feed all of us. So to help with that, my cousins and I would wake up early in the morning and go out to collect cans and bottles, then cash them in to get money. We would give each other Entenmann's cake parties in the back of my grandmother's building. One time we had to eat the cookies we brought for a party for dinner. During the summer months, we would wake up early to walk to different schools in the neighborhood that still offered free breakfast and lunch.

One day as my mother was heading out to the store, I walked to the window and looked outside, wishing I could go with her. I saw her go over to a man. He gave her something, and she gave him money. While we were staying at my grandmother's house, my mom would sometimes tell me and my siblings that we'd all go shopping together after school. We would come home happy, thinking about that treat. Then we'd look around for our mother only to find out she had left early that morning—and sometimes she didn't return until days later. One day, I found my mother's crack pipe in the sofa—her bed at my grandmother's house.

A couple of months later, we moved into a shelter. By this time, my mother had four children—three girls and one boy. While we were there, my mother got a settlement from a lawsuit she had filed from falling on the job; she worked as a home attendant. Eventually, we got a four-bedroom apartment in Harlem. We only lived there for a little while before my mother started smoking again. I can still remember one time when my mother went running down the block with my aunts chasing her. I'm not exactly sure why they were chasing her, but next thing I knew one of my aunts took us back to my grandmother's house.

My older sister and I went to go visit my mother not too long after that, and when we walked in the house, we were shocked to see all the tv's were gone. When we walked into her bedroom, she was sitting on her bed in front of a table full of crack. My baby sister was behind her. I was scared and nervous. My sister flushed the crack down the toilet, grabbed my little sister, and we ran out of the house. We didn't stop running until we got to the bus stop. Luckily for us the bus was there, and we got on the bus heading towards our grandmother's house. A few weeks later, my mother lost that apartment. Once again, we were back in the shelter. I remember being in EAU (which was the shelter) and sleeping on chairs pushed together. All of us slept on chairs except my baby sister, who had a crib. We were living in Brooklyn at this time, and we stayed there for a couple of months My older sibling and I had to commute to Manhattan, though, where we still attended school.

One day we returned from school to find out that our mother was missing. Some lady who slept near us in the shelter was holding my little sister. She said that our mother had left that morning and asked her to watch the baby. My mother never returned, though, so the lady had to take us downstairs to some office. When we moved into our temporary housing in the shelter, my mother wrote a letter that they had on file, saying if anything was to happen to her, they should give us to my aunt. We reached my grandmother and she came out there to get us, but the administrators wouldn't give us to her—only to my aunt.

Eventually the problem of custody got sorted out and we went to go live with our aunt, who lived in New Jersey. She worked in the city, though, and we still went to school in Harlem. ACS told my aunt she would have to move into the city with us. We stayed in Jersey for a few months, then we moved to a two-bedroom apartment in the Bronx, on the Grand Concourse. It was different living with my aunt—she ran a very strict household. My aunt didn't have any children at the time, and it was a little difficult for her to adjust to parenthood. As for my mother, she enrolled in a rehab program to get herself clean. We lived with my aunt for a couple of months, but it was a struggle financially. My aunt would go to the supermarket with pennies to get food for us.

Months later, my mother returned. We had just gotten back from school one day, and we walked in to see her sitting on the couch in the living room. Later that same day, our aunt told us we would be going back to live with our mother. That day also happened to be my oldest sister's birthday. We went back to the shelter with my mother—this time we were placed in Manhattan. Once we were settled into the shelter, we also found out that my mother was pregnant. My oldest brother was very upset. Even as children, we knew the last thing we needed in our situation was another baby. We were barely making it as it was, and it was a struggle for me and my siblings to perform day-to-day tasks like washing clothes and putting together a decent meal. Adding another mouth was only going to make it harder.

As a child, I remember crying to my older siblings for things whenever we took the train to school. They put up with a lot. I cried because I wanted the cookies or candy from a little corner store next to the train station. I would ask my older siblings every morning whether I could have the candy; they would tell me no, because they didn't have any money. I cried because of that. On the train, my sister use to tell me, "I'm tired of your mother paying us in food stamps to babysit you." Since I was younger, I couldn't know that she and my older brother were actually embarrassed by my outbursts because other riders could hear them say we didn't have any money.

Finally, we moved out of the shelter and into an apartment in Manhattan. My mom, my three siblings, and I moved to 128th Street and Madison

Avenue. By that time, I was in junior high school—
in the sixth grade, to be exact. Things were okay for
a year or so. My mother gave birth to a little boy.
He was so cute! I was happy for a little while. Then,
in seventh grade, my life took an unexpected turn
for the worse.

I remember clearly that it was the first of the
month. Normally, my mother would give each of us
fifty dollars, so we could buy our personal items for
the entire month. I was expecting that money, and I
needed to wash my clothes and buy some feminine
products. We came home from school asking for the
money, but my mother told us that she got robbed
coming out of the check-cashing place with my
younger siblings. We just looked at her and walked
away.

On a cool fall day not long after that, I was

walking home from school tired. I just wanted to go home and get a good night's rest. When I walked into our apartment, my mother's boyfriend (and my little sister's father) was sitting on the couch playing with my little sister. He was very nice at first—he bought me a teddy bear and other small treats. But when my sister turned four, he started drinking and smoking. His attitude changed. He started yelling at us. He was using drugs, and he was an alcoholic. He used to call me all kinds of names and say I was stupid because I did not speak Spanish. I came home one day to find that he had sold all my clothes. That night, my siblings and I slept in a twin-size bed together because we were scared of him.

My mother started going to my little sister's aunt's house and staying there for months at a time.

She would only take my little brother and little sister with her. She left me and my older siblings behind in the apartment. She would not call or come to check on us for months. I remember washing my clothes by hand and hanging them in front of the oven overnight to dry. I didn't have any money to wash my clothes, so this was how I cleaned them for school. We ate whatever there was to eat and didn't complain. Even though my mom was not there, though, we still went to school. My mother didn't teach us any life skills—how to clean up. We were kids and we did the best we could to maintain the house while she was gone. She never came to school for parent-teacher conferences, either. I remember looking at the other kids and their parents, wishing she would be there. Every day in the seventh grade, all my friends would go to the store and buy food before we got on the train. I would just stand there, watching them, because I had no money. I would go around in the apartment building we lived in, knocking on doors of neighbors asking if they needed anything from the store; I'd charge them five dollars to run their errands, so I would have money for an upcoming trip or just to have some pocket money for school.

One of my friends in junior high had a stable home and parents who loved her, and I realize now that part of my learning how to be a mom myself came from watching other people's mothers. Our neighbor upstairs also showed me how to be a mother. Her husband got killed, so she had to raise four children on her own. She did an excellent job as a single parent, and I watched her. She took us to church and bought me clothes. I appreciated everything.

Shortly after that, my mother's boyfriend told my mother he wanted us out of the house. Clearly, she would do whatever he told her to, so our own mother told us we had to get out. She called the cops and told them to take us to my grandmother's house. I had missed seventy-two days of school in the eighth grade, so I got held back because my mother boyfriend kept me up at night yelling, cursing, and drinking. When my birthday came around, I was at my grandmother's house again. I didn't want anything but for my mother to call me and say, "happy birthday." She never called.

The only thing our mother ever really taught us about how to live was how to budget, because we had to stretch that fifty dollars, she gave us every month. If my cousins or I told my grandmother we were hungry, she would reply, "Did you fucking see *me* eat today?" When she did give us money to eat, it was only ever about two dollars. I love my grandmother, though, and believe she did her best. One night my cousin and I stayed outside late. When we came back, our aunt started yelling at us and saying we were "too fuckin' grown" for that and she "hoped we got raped."

August of 1997, someone called ACS on my grandmother. We all were removed from my grandmother's apartment and placed with my aunt. My grandmother knew it had to have been somebody from the family who turned us in because of details that were given on the ACS report. Whoever called ACS called my cousin by her nickname. My aunt had a one-bedroom apartment, but there were eight of us living there. We all slept in the living room.

Living with my aunt was hectic. Whoever was on the big sofa first got to sleep on it. The rest of us slept were we could. I lived with my aunt for about two months before I got really tired of it. One day I had just come in from school and I wanted to take a quick shower. While I was in the shower, my aunt came in the bathroom and started yelling at me, asking why I was in the shower and why I didn't know her husband had been about to get in. I said, "I didn't know he was getting in the shower! You want me to get out?" She said yes, so I got out and let him get in. When he was finished, I got back in. I started crying in there because I was tired of so many people. I couldn't take it anymore, so I left. I was fourteen.

My older sister had gotten her own apartment by then, and she let me move in with her. I didn't have anything—no clothes, nothing. My sister gave me all of her clothes she had. It felt good to finally have some decent clothes on. Later on, that school year, I started dating a really nice young man. He was very kind to me. Being that almost everyone else in my life was so mean to me, this was very foreign. It was different being treated nicely. It was puppy love—he bought me presents, and I bought him presents. It was cute. We eventually went to the prom together. I didn't have enough money to get a dress, so I wore my sister's old prom dress—and I had to wear her graduation dress as well. I was happy, though, and it was nice.

I only graduated junior high because of my age, not my grades. When the test results came back, I saw that I had failed. I'm not complaining. I had gone through a lot. With losing my mother, I could not focus on what was happening in class, and I didn't really care about the test. My aunt learned that I had only gotten a score of two on the math test, so she told everyone that I was dumb. I knew I wasn't dumb—I just wanted my mother.

The summer after junior high school, I lost my virginity to the boy I had been seeing. We continued to date even though we went to different high schools. He was my first love. The distance proved to be too much, though, and our relationship went downhill. We broke up the next year. I started dating someone else from my high school; he was nice and polite too. He took me shopping, and every night we went out to eat dinner or to the movies— whatever I wanted to do.

When our relationship started getting very serious, we both thought it was time to meet each other's parents and families. His mother was very nice, and I think because she only had sons, she treated me like I was her daughter. We did everything together, like getting our hair, nails, and toes done.

Whenever his parents took him and his brothers shopping, they took me shopping as well. Things were going well between us. I could finally say that I was happy and that I had a family.

A couple of months later, I found out I was pregnant. I was in my second year of high school. I didn't know what I was going to do. I asked him what he planned on doing about it. He said, "Nothing. What *can* I do?"

By the time I really felt like I was pregnant,

I felt different. We had an argument about what to do, so I said I'd go to the doctor to make sure everything was okay before we decided. They gave me a paper saying I was pregnant. I gave it to his mother and left.

I went home to my sister's house. I didn't know what I was going to do—I was only sixteen years old. His mother and father called later that night and asked me to keep the baby. His mother said that they would help me with the baby. I heard his father in the background saying, "I will do anything and everything for my grandchild." That shocked me a little, because I didn't know his father knew English. Every time we had gone out together, my boyfriend and his brothers had spoken to their father in Spanish. His mother also told me, "Don't worry about the baby. We will take care of our grandchild, just take care of yourself." I thanked them and told them I still had a lot to think about.

I eventually told my sister, and my heart dropped when I did. I also told her I didn't know what I wanted to do—have the baby, or get an abortion? In the end, I decided to keep the baby. During my pregnancy, I was very mean to my son's grandmother. I also stopped liking my baby father's and his brothers. Before my pregnancy, I loved my boyfriend's mother's cooking. It was delicious. While I was pregnant, though, I couldn't stand the smell of her food. She tried to be nice about it. Whenever she went food shopping for the house, she gave me a separate shopping cart just for me and told me to get whatever I wanted to eat. They took me out to eat every Friday. They took me wherever I wanted to go. I technically lived with my sister, but I was at my son's father's house all the time.

It was strange being pregnant. I felt my son moving and kicking *all* the time. I was mad most of the pregnancy. I don't know why. Maybe because by that time it had been about three years since I had spoken to my mother. My boyfriend's family took good care of me. They even threw me a spectacular baby shower—it was so nice. They even had to rent a U-Haul van to bring my gifts home from the shower, I got so many. They said to me don't get mad everything is going to be nice at the party I was going to, but it was the baby shower.

On May 18, 2000, I gave birth to my son. He was 8 pounds, 1 ounce, and 21 inches. The birth was pretty quick. My water broke at seven in the morning at my boyfriend's house. I went to the hospital at 7:30 a.m. and gave birth at 10:36 a.m. My son's father was there, and his mother. I got an epidural once I was dilated to six centimeters, so my body was numb for a little while after the delivery was over. When I left the hospital three days later, I went home to my sister's house. I stopped by my boyfriend's parents' house first.

For the first month that my son was here, I cried every night because the baby cried. I think he was constipated because of the milk. His father was there with us and he tried to help, but he didn't know what to do either. He still did his best, and that was very thoughtful of him. He used to leave and go to his mother house to get some sleep, though, and I was mad I couldn't get sleep of my own. His parents still take care of my son to this day.

At that same time, my mother came back in the picture. Her boyfriend was in jail and she had another baby. My mother had six children total: three boys and three girls. Being that my mother's boyfriend was in prison, my older sister and I helped take care of my youngest siblings—two boys and one girl.

My son's father and I stayed together till my son was one going on two years old. When my son was about fourteen months old, I went on vacation to Disney World with my sister and my son's godmother. I needed a vacation, because I had a fight with a girl who said my son's father took her virginity and only bought her some Pepe jeans. I told her that's all she was going to get. While I was in the relationship with my son's father, he took care of me. Whenever he got paid, he gave me half.

But we had problems as well. He was outside all the time. After I had the fight with the first girl, it seemed like every week I heard something about him being with other girls. One day I cried because he never spent any time with me anymore, and he would come home late. I had to tell myself, "What are you crying for? He's going to do what he wants whether you cry or not." After having that fight with the girl, I thought about going back to fight her again—but she was fourteen and I was eighteen. I had to be careful. I could go to jail for fighting a minor, and then who was going to take care of my son? So, I left and went on vacation to Disney World for seven days instead.

Disney World was amazing. My son was excited—he loved all the Disney characters. I was excited as well. I had never been to Florida. The park was amazing, and huge. We stopped at one of the gift shops in the park because I wanted to bring back some gifts for my son's grandmother. My sister, my son's godmother, and I decided to take the key chains instead of paying for them, though. When we tried to walk out of the gift shop with the items, a security guard stopped us and asked us if he could see what was in the stroller. When he pulled the bag out from the back of the stroller, all the key chains were there. The park took the items back, but they made me sign a paper that I would never return to the Magic Kingdom again. I didn't.

When we came home after that, my son's father was disrespectful. He called me all kinds of bitch names. I told him I'd be a bitch—but not *his* bitch. When he would call me all those names, I would get mad enough to call his mother a bitch, and I said that with her standing right there. He clearly did not appreciate me as a person. I had to go. I was over the disrespectful treatment, and I told myself I couldn't be out there, fighting his other girls. I was thinking to myself, "If I fight this little girl, then I'm going to have to fight every girl that he deals with. That's not going to happen. I have to live life for me and my son." To top it off, just before I had the fight with that girl, I found out he'd slept with someone else too. I even knew the girl— we grew up on the same block. How could I be mad at her if I wasn't mad at him? She did not put a gun to his head and say, "Fuck me." He did it because he wanted to. He did not care about me.

After this situation, I started dating somebody I met through a friend. He was nice. He had a job, and no kids. He was different from my son's father and my first love. He was young, but he was nice too. He called me every day, and he would even leave songs on my voice mail. I started to really like him.

I would tell my son's father I had something to do so I could go see him. We dated for about six months, but that was it. One day I was at my friend's house because things weren't right at home. My son's father and I were always arguing. Things were not okay with my living situation. Living with my sister, I remember whenever I would bring my son to the house and he would be crying she would say, "You know I have to go to work. This baby is crying, so shut him up."

So, on that note, I only took him to her house about every two months. I stayed mostly at my son's father's house. I also remember being nine months pregnant and my sister got my welfare check. It was for sixty-two dollars. She gave me ten dollars of it and sent the rest of the money to *her* boyfriend. She told me my baby's father should make sure I had money. Another day when I was at my sister's house, she came home with some clothes for a little baby boy. I said "Aww," put the clothes to my stomach, and said, "My son is going to look cute in this." She replied, "That's not for *your* baby."

Some months went by, and my son was about six months old. I let my sister file taxes for my son. She gave me $300 and said to me if it weren't for her he would not have anything. Not only did I watch *her* daughter overnight while she worked, I also took her to school in the morning, I had to drop her off and pick her up from the babysitter as well. Lucky for me her babysitter wasn't too far away from my high school. I had to leave her apartment. I felt like my only real option was to go live in the shelter. I didn't know if I ever wanted to have another baby. How could I have a second baby, if we could barely afford the child we had now? I went in the shelter not knowing what to expect. I remember praying to God, asking him to guide me on the right path so I could get my own apartment. I was eighteen, and my son was one.

My sister came to the shelter, crying and telling me I didn't have to stay there. My son's grandparents told me as well that they would get me an apartment, but I said no. I wanted to stay there and get my own place for me and my son. This was the only way I knew how to accomplish that. Besides, I thought, "If something happens to my son's father, what will I do?" Being in an apartment where my son's father was paying for everything wouldn't work if he got hurt or something. At that point, I did not want to be with him anymore anyway.

I had to do this on my own.

3 MISTAKES

I had been in the shelter for about four months when I heard that my first boyfriend's best friend was murdered. I called his house—the number was the same as when we were in junior high school. He didn't believe it was me on the phone. He was asking questions like, "Is this really Alexis Moreira? You have a son?" We reconnected immediately, and from there we started talking about what had happened to us over the years. He knew I still was with my son's father, but also that I was on the way out of that relationship. At the time, he had a girlfriend—but he told me he didn't.

I worked at White Castle during the evenings, so I told the shelter I had to work overnight as an excuse to stay out. I stayed with my first boyfriend at his house. It was nice, going back to my first boyfriend. After I had my son, I had started smoking weed. My first boyfriend smoked as well, so that's what we did.

After about three months of dating with him, my son's father found out about me and my first boyfriend. My son's father's friends had also seen me and my first boyfriend together. I had found out in the meantime that my first *did* have a girlfriend, because he was telling me a story once about something he'd said to her—clearly, he'd forgotten he told me he did *not* have a girlfriend.

It was starting to get crazy. I was in love with my first boyfriend, and I didn't know what I wanted to do with these guys. One day, I went to my son's father's house directly after leaving my first boyfriend's house. He had given me a few hickeys on my chest, and I didn't realize it. I was sitting on the couch and when my son's father saw the hickeys, he went crazy. He put my clothes in a pall with my phone. He broke my glasses, broke the phone charger, and slapped the shit out of me. He said he was going to burn all my stuff and said, "I paid for this shit!" I still stayed with my first boyfriend—I loved him, and he was my friend. I knew in due time I would have to decide between the two.

One day, my son's father and I had an argument. He came to my job to talk to me. My boss let me go home early. So, he went to my first boyfriend's house. He seen me with my first, and he asked if he could talk to us. We said okay. My son's father put his hand around my first boyfriend's neck. My first boyfriend said, "Get the fuck off me." They were in each other's faces, so I got in the middle of them. My son's father punched my boyfriend in the face. They started fighting harder, and I was in the middle. They were swinging on each other, trying not to hit me. They each had like three friends with them, so everybody was fighting. It was crazy.

After the fight, I went and stood on the corner, waiting to go upstairs with my first boyfriend. My son's father came up, threw me over his shoulder, and put me in the car. He turned on the child safety lock, so I couldn't get out. I started fighting him when I realized I couldn't get out of the car, but he was in the front seat and I was in the

41

back seat. He was driving around trying, to get something to hurt my boyfriend. He never got it, though.

I spoke with my first boyfriend the next day. His family and friends were telling him to stay away from me. He said it was not my fault they had a fight, and so we stayed together. I was with both of them still, but I knew I would have to choose who I was going to be with. I didn't do it right away, but a couple of months later I did make my decision: I stayed with my junior high boyfriend—my friend, my honeybun. I loved him.

During the six months I was in the shelter, I had taken a training program, so I would be able to open up my own day care in my apartment (once I got one). The course was free, and I completed it. I was cleared by the state to deal with children. This was a plan B for my life. I wasn't sure where I was going with my life, but I knew God had me. The whole time I was in the shelter, my older sister got welfare for me and my son. My son's grandparents and his father also took care of us while we were in the shelter. I had a job—it was nothing important, but I was earning my own money.

In my relationship with my honeybun, he was nice. He was the same as my son's father, but different. That means they both gave me whatever I asked for, but my honeybun had respect for me. He was more affectionate, and he would always tell me he loved me. With my son's father, I remember asking him all the time if he loved me. We continued on with the relationship—me and my honeybun.

I was still smoking at this point, and my son was three years old. I told myself I wanted a career. I knew smoking weed would not fit in with that dream, so I stopped. I had been smoking every day, almost *all* day. I wanted a change in my life, and I wanted to set an example for my son. I didn't want him to see me like that. I prayed to God and asked him to help me, help me to stop smoking, and to please give me a better life. I recognized that I was doing the same thing my mother had done to me and my siblings. I had to leave that alone. I did it. I usually smoked with a couple of people, but when I stopped we went in different directions.

I got a job working as a security guard. It was okay at first, but once I saw how the owners did business, I realized it was *not* good. I worked there

for about three years, but I hated that job because

the bosses were always hitting on me and I didn't

like it. I told myself, "Don't mess with people you

work with." And, by the way, I also had a

boyfriend. I wanted to quit every time I went to

work. But I couldn't, because of my son. I had to

feed him. His father had gotten into trouble, so I had

to take care of my son. I had a lot of support from

my son's grandmother, so I never had to look for a

babysitter. She was always there for us. I loved her.

His grandparents still help me take care of him

today.

The job didn't pay much, but some money is

better than nothing. I worked as a security guard

only on the weekend; during the week I would

babysit with the certification I got to open a daycare in my apartment. I also decided to enroll in college in the spring semester of 2005. I wanted more out of life, and I knew going to school was the key. No one could take your education away from you. I completed my classes the first semester. While I was still in school, I started taking home health aide classes. About three weeks into that program, they called me in a room and said, "You told us you had never been convicted of a crime." I said I've never been convicted of a crime, and they said, "So why does a warrant come up for your arrest in Orange County, Florida, for robbery?" I said I didn't know.

My older sister had been paying monthly to keep a lawyer's services. So, I called the lawyer services, and they said, "Don't stay in your house."

This was the situation from Disney World again. Even though they got their merchandise back—and it was only $150 worth of stuff to begin with. They had also added my sister's and my son's godmother's items to my charge. I hadn't been the only one stealing, but when they couldn't show a receipt for what they had bought, the park put all the stuff on me. I went out to eat that night with my honeybun. We talked about the warrant and went home.

The next morning around six o'clock, someone started banging on the door. They came into the house asking me if I knew my son's father. Then they asked my honeybun and me for our IDs. I knew I was going to jail. They ran the ID and said, "You have to come with us." The two officers didn't put handcuffs on me as we walked out of my building to the cop car that was in the front of my building. I went to the precinct, and they put me in a cell. The officer was nice enough to turn the TV on for me and to give me soda with some peanut M&Ms. They took me to central booking, and then after a while they took me straight to the third floor, so I could see the judge quick.

I went to the Rose M. Singer Center on Rikers Island—the jail for women in Queens. It was horrible. I was there for a month. When I first got there, I was scared because I did not know what to expect. I was in general population, and every day I would read this little Bible that I had. One night, I felt free. I had a dream that I was going home. In it, they called my name and said, "Alexis Moreira, you're going home." I grabbed all of my belongings and ran out of my jail cell so damn fast... only to wake up the next morning and realize that it was only a dream. *FUCK.*

I wasn't scared, though. I told myself I couldn't let those bitches see me sweat. I talked to a couple of people, but I mostly kept to myself. They moved me to a different house at one point. When I got there, I went to my cell to put my stuff away. It was hot in there, but I said to myself, "I'm not getting in the shower with these girls. I don't want anyone looking at me." That thought went out the window quickly—it was *so* hot. I took a shower, and it was awkward, but I was hot, so I figured, "Oh well."

I stayed to myself. Whenever people would

ask me what I was in there for, I would say I did not want to talk about it. I remember meeting a cellmate and she was nice. We went to church together. I would use the phone in the morning in the afternoon and at night—three times a day. Talking to my honeybun and my family. I called my son, but not a lot because that's what made me cry. I told him I took a job in Florida and I would be back soon. I knew he was safe with his grandmother.

I had a friend that I met in junior high school—when I started dating my honeybun—who said she would help me with my situation. My honeybun could not come see me, because he couldn't visit any one in jail. He had gone to see another friend in jail months earlier, and he had weed in his pocket. That meant he was banned from visitation. So, my honeybun would drive other people to the jail to visit me and wait in the parking lot for them. I spoke to him daily, but I could only see him when I went to court.

I went to court twice during that month. The first time, I thought it meant I was going home so I gave all my clothes away to another lady in jail. My honeybun had to buy the stuff I needed all over again. He also gave me money for commissary—for whatever I wanted, books, etc. He paid all the bills for my apartment and got me a lawyer. He made us pay $2,000 and then he did not do anything because the case was based in Florida. We only found out *after* Honeybun paid the money to the lawyer that he wouldn't be able to help us.

While in jail, I kept reading the Bible. The

only time I left the cell was to go to church. One day, a woman decided she was going to try me. I was taking a shower, and this girl said, "Today is my birthday. Will you come outside with me?" That was a code for eating each other out. A third inmate would look out for the guards while they were in the cell, playing with each other. I said no. She said, "You are going tell me no even though it's my birthday?" I said yes. I got out of the shower and went to my cell to get dressed. A fellow cellmate came in my cell and asked again: "You not coming out with us?" I told her no, and she left. I think if I would have gone with them, they would have done me dirty. Being that I was able to tell the girls no, they knew I was not scared of them. I just minded my own business. I'd see them fighting for the phones, but I didn't even look at them. I could care less.

When I used to walk the halls in jail, the guards used to say, "What are you doing here?"

4 ALL THESE SURPRISES

One day, a corrections officer came to get me from my jail cell to escort me to court. My family was sitting in the courtroom, next to the sheriffs. The judge told me I would have to settle my case in Florida. The officer led me out of the court with handcuffs on my hands, around my waist, and around my ankles. He put me in a van. It was all guys in the van—I was the only woman. My family was standing outside crying, and I started crying too.

They took everyone in the van to a jail in New Jersey overnight, so they could get rest because they were driving us to Florida. I was in a holding cell, which meant I had to sleep on the floor with just a wool blanket. It was crazy, because I was at the end of my menstrual period, I didn't even have pads. I also couldn't take a bath. Or brush my teeth. They gave the inmates cookies and juice. My hair had started falling out when I was in jail on Rikers Island, and I had lost weight. It was degrading for me to be in this situation. We had to stop at court in Brooklyn to pick up another inmate who had to be extradited to Florida too. The next morning, we drove to Florida.

By the time I got there, my honeybun and friend were waiting for me. My bail was set at $5,000, or in bail bonds, $500. The Florida jail was different from the jail in New York City. This jail had air-conditioning, and you were put in a room with six people, a toilet, and a free phone. On Rikers Island it was one phone for about thirty women, and it was not free. A girl in Florida called home and did a three-way call for me. I called my honeybun, and learned he was already trying to bail me out when I called him. He would have to pay the whole $5,000 because I was not a resident of Florida. They could not just pay for the bail bonds because we needed collateral in Florida; if I couldn't get the whole bail amount together, I would not be able to go back to New York City.

My older sister, my honeybun, my aunt, and my cousin put up the bail money. My sister put up the most—$4,400. My honeybun put in $500, and my aunt and cousin $150. I had four charges: robbery in the second degree, resistance merchandise, battery, and petty theft. I didn't even see the judge while I was in jail in Florida. Being that the whole $5,000 was paid, I was supposed to be able to return to the city.

At four o'clock in the morning, the guard called me to come out of the room. I thought I was leaving. I woke up and started getting my things together. She said, "What are you doing? You're going to see your lawyer. You're not going home." The guard escorted me to a small room, and I saw my lawyer sitting there. I was praying he had some good news for me. During the conversation with my lawyer, he told me I should plea "no contest" so I could go home. The only hitch of pleading that would mean I would have a misdemeanor on my record. I agreed to the plea deal only so I could get the hell out of jail and go home to my son.

Two hours after I spoke with my lawyer, the guard called my name and said, "Let's go Ms. Moreira. You're going home." My heart dropped. I was so damn happy to get out of there. They had called my honeybun and my friend to come and get me. I was sitting in the front of the jail, putting my shoelaces in my shoes, and my honeybun ran in the jail and hugged me. I hadn't seen him for the whole month while I was in jail. I had to get permission saying that it was okay for me to fly back to the city. My honeybun had paid to come with my friend to Florida: hotel, airfare, food, and my bail with the bail bonds. Once the judge gave me permission to fly back to New York, I was so happy that I could finally go home to my family and my son.

When Honeybun and I got back to the city, we had no money. We were both broke. My honeybun's friend gave him $200 to help us get through the situation. I started working as a security guard and babysitting during the week again.

Even though I was back in New York, I knew I would still have to appear in court in Florida. Monday morning, I called the courthouse I had last appeared in while I was in Florida. A representative told me I had an upcoming court appearance on Wednesday. I had less than twenty-four hours to get my ass back to Florida—or I'm going back to jail. The representative also told me that I had another court appearance next week Thursday as well. My friend and I left from JFK airport the next morning. At the first court hearing, the judge told me that if I decided to go to trial and the jury find me guilty. I could get up to fifteen years in jail. The judge also stated that the State of Florida was still charging me with all four counts, which were felonies. The last court hearing I attended in Florida, the state decided to drop the charges down to petty theft. Which is a misdemeanor. As a result of the state dropping the charges down to a misdemeanor I had probation, anger management courses, and community service for one year.

The State of Florida tried to tell me that there was a chance New York might not accept my probation terms. So, there was a chance I would have to move to Florida to complete my probation. My honeybun said, "If you have to come out here to live for a year, I'm coming with you."

When I got back to New York City after my last court hearing, I discovered I was pregnant. The next weekend, I was bleeding and had bad cramps, so we went to the emergency room. I went to the bathroom at one point and there was no toilet paper. I was bleeding a lot, so my honeybun took his shirt off and gave it to me, so I could clean myself from using the bathroom. The following Tuesday, my honeybun and I went to a sonogram appointment— our first one to check on the baby. When they did the sonogram, they discovered the baby had no heart beat. I had a miscarriage. I got up off the sonogram table and my honeybun just hugged me and said, "I'm sorry."

I got a job working at my college as a security guard. I started probation, but my anger management courses and community service had not started yet. As I stated above, my older sister and my son's godmother had been stealing in Florida too, but I did not tell on them when I got caught. My son's godmother never came to court, called, or showed any support for me going to jail for what all of us had done. I never said anything to her about not being there. One of the kids that I was babysitting was her youngest son. When I came home, she lied to me and told me she had stopped getting her ACD, so I did not have to watch him anymore. Somewhere down the line, she slipped up and told me who was babysitting the baby and receiving the ACD. I didn't say anything.

During my second semester of college I was granted work study. I started babysitting during the day and went to school in the evening. My honey bun would watch the kids during their nap time while I got dress for school. When I would get paid, he would say, "Keep the money for the bills."

I had been working for about three months when I applied for a case management job. They called me back for an interview, and I got it. I was able to stop babysitting, quit work study and my weekend job as a security. This was my first salary base job with real benefits such as time off with pay and medical insurance. This job paid enough money that I would only have to work one job. I was happy. I was twenty-two years old, driving, in college, and working as a case manager. This was the end of 2005.

I had decided to let my son go to elementary school near where his grandmother lived because I had to work and go to school, and I needed to know he would be okay. Someone to pick him up from school, take him to school—all of the above.

In January of 2006, the doctors had told me that I had cancer cells in my cervix. I decided to have surgery to remove the cancerous cells. I remember going to my honeybun's grandmother's house and crying as I told him. He said, "Don't worry, Boo. You will be okay." The doctor had told me that there was a chance it might not heal correctly after the surgery, that I would not be able to have any more children, and that the cancer cells might come back. When I woke up from the surgery, my honeybun was standing in front of me.

I continued to work at the case management job. About a month later, my mother announced that she wanted her boyfriend out of her house—my little sister's father. I was at work, and my mother called me saying she was going to kill him. I left work, so we could all meet up—I worked just a couple of blocks from her house. My older sister and I went to the apartment with my mother and the kids. My honeybun met us down there after he got off work. It was crazy. We asked my mother's boyfriend to leave. While we were asking him to go he called the cops and told them my honeybun had a gun. He called his family as well, and they came with people to fight us. He eventually left—and took everything but the can opener. He left my mother and younger siblings with nothing. He took *everything*: the couches, kitchen table, TVs, computer, the cable, dishes, pots. Everything.

I let my mother stay in my apartment. Since I only had one bedroom, we were cramped up for a week. My older sister and I went back to my mother's apartment, painted it, and put everything back in. We got sofas, a kitchen table, TVs, dishes, a computer, pictures for the walls, and everything else they needed. We went half and half on putting the stuff back in the house. When we took my mother back home with the kids, everything was there. She did not know we were doing that, and she was so happy she kissed both of us.

Once my mother's boyfriend was out of the picture, my older sister and I started taking care of our younger siblings. I worked from paycheck to paycheck to make sure my mother and siblings were okay. Later on, that year, my sister and I went to the Poconos to get a house, so we could all live together. That had never happened before—my mother and all of her kids living together. My older sister's credit was good, so we bought the house in her name.

I was still working as a case manager, on probation, doing anger management on the weekend, community service, and in school full-time. In the midst of all this, I still took care of myself and my son. I could even get my hair done and go out to eat—whatever I wanted to do. I remember telling my sister I was still planning to give her money for the house. Sometime later, she started flipping out. She was cursing, yelling, and saying she was tired of people. She said she didn't understand how we were going shopping and spending money when the down payment for the house was due.

It was almost the end of my probation, and I gave my sister $1500 for the house's closing. I completed my community service—where I had to serve food to homeless people—and taking my anger management classes. The probation officer told me that I still owed money to the courts in Florida and that if I did not pay I would have to stay on probation until I could. It was about $860. I didn't know what to do. I did not have it. My honeybun gave me the money to pay off Florida and gave me half of the money for the down payment.

Finally, I was off probation. It was September of 2006. My older sister and I went to a car dealership. We both wanted new cars. My credit wasn't so good but hers was, so the dealer told her to put both cars in her name. She said no. For me to get a new car, I would have to trade in my 1991 Honda Accord and leave a down payment of $3,000. I called my honeybun, and he gave me the money.

My honeybun drove me to work every morning, picked me up after work, drove me to school, and picked me up from school—my friends *and* me. I worked in Harlem, just a couple of blocks from my mother's apartment. So, on the days I had the car, I would leave my car with my mother and walk to work.

Twice a month, we drove up to the Poconos to see the progress on the house being built. I continued to work and go to school and take care of my mother and siblings. I remember we were taking my siblings to get sneakers, and I had stopped in The Children's Place. I picked up some tennis dresses for my goddaughter while I was there; my sister said I was always buying her something.

In December 2006, my honeybun got arrested. His bail was set at $8,000. I went to his grandmother's house after court to see what they were going to do about it. The brother said he was going to go to my honeybun's friend's in a little while. I looked at him and just got up and went to the friend's myself. I asked him for the number to two of his other friends. Altogether, I collected $4,500. I called his father and asked him if he could put up the rest. He said yes. I went and bailed him out.

The next week, someone called my job. It was a female, and she left a message on my coworker's phone extension. The person said, "This message is for Alexis Moreira. Thank you for bailing my honeybun out of jail. I called The Boat and they told me he got bailed out. Thank you for being on your job. Now my baby can have a father"

I called Honeybun and asked him, "Do you have a baby?" He said, "No, I don't have a baby. What are you talking about?" I told him someone called my job and I told him what she said. I asked him a few times more after the first talk. I wanted to give him the opportunity to tell me honestly, so I could determine if I wanted to stay in the relationship. He continued to say no—but that's something I could not have expected. Was he really having his first kid outside of our relationship? My coworker was amazed at how I handled the situation. I didn't trip, get mad, or lose my mind at what that girl said. I felt like losing it wouldn't change the situation. The baby was still coming, if that was the truth. After asking him so much, I knew what I was going to do if, down the line, the baby did come. I would leave when I found out, because it would mean he lied. He also told me he wouldn't hide his kids and he would never do that for anyone—not even me.

5 IT'S TIME FOR CHANGE

Within the next couple of months, I applied for a job at a preschool. The interview went so well that they offered me the position on the spot. After I accepted the preschool teaching position. When I went to work the next day at my case managing job, I put in my two weeks and started at the preschool the following Monday. The preschool job was located in the Bronx which was a plus for me because I didn't have to travel to Harlem. I worked in my niece's school. She was even in my class. She never made a mistake and called me Auntie—she called me "Ms. Moreira." It was cute. A month into working at the preschool, I found out I was pregnant. I called Honeybun and told him. He was happy, but I was stressed. I was tired every day after work. I went home and slept—that's it.

The house was almost finished. My sister and I went half and half on the costs of furnishings. We also went shopping at Home Depot and Target to get house things. One day, my niece's father brought her to school. He said, "Let me talk to you. Are you okay? Because your sister told me your boyfriend is stressing you out and that's why you don't come around anymore." I said, "Why would she tell you that? That's not true, but I do need to talk to her to see what we can do as far as the bills. I need help saving money because I'm about to have another baby." Later on, when he came to pick his daughter up, he said to me, "We could turn your room in the house into the guest room." I just looked at him. He told me, "How could you be with somebody that can't do anything for you? For me, as a man, I provided for my family." I started crying and walked to my car.

Honeybun was there to pick me up. When I went to the car, Honeybun said, "What happened?" I said I was feeling sick and tired because of the baby. We went home, and I called my sister three times to talk to her about helping me save money for the baby. She did not pick up.

Later, I spoke to my son god mother. She told me that my sister was flipping out. Her daughter's father went and told her that I said I didn't want to be part of the new house anymore, and she believed him and stopped talking to me.

I was stressed about the baby. I didn't know if I wanted it. I prayed to God and spoke to him, saying, "I don't have money to take care of this baby. I don't think I'm ready. Help me, God. You

74

know I am going to keep this baby, because you will never put more on me than I can handle. I would love a girl, but just give me a healthy baby."

I never told Honeybun what happened between my sister and I to this very day. Why I did not go to Pennsylvania. They moved to the Poconos, but I didn't go. I continued to work at the preschool. Honeybun would cook lunch for me and bring it to my job, and we would eat in the car. He would bring me a quart of milk to drink so the baby would grow healthy. That was cute.

About a month later, I decided to go back to the case management job because the preschool did not pay me what they said they were going to pay me. I looked at my first check and asked to speak to the supervisor. By the time I got to speak to her, I had already called my old job and set up an interview for a position higher than the position I was in before I left; I had more credits by then. I went for the interview and got the job.

From time to time, my mother would call me, but not a lot. My older nieces told my sister that when I spoke to them on the phone I spoke to everybody *except* for my sister's two daughters. That was a lie—I spoke to everyone. My older sister told my mother and younger sibling that they could not call me from her phone, but that was the only phone they had. So, I couldn't speak to them anymore.

Because I did not go with them to the Poconos, I went to Target and bought new things for my apartment in the city. I needed to see a change.

That same month, Honeybun was sentenced

to go to jail. He would have to be there eight months, and I was four months pregnant. This was in August 2007.

I started to get ready for my baby shower. I didn't know what gender the baby was, because during my first sonogram the baby covered its eyes and closed its legs. I didn't find out that she was a girl until I was eight months along. I had issue with my balance when I was pregnant, which I told the doctor. She said sometimes that happened while you are pregnant.

One day, I had gone to Honeybun's mother's house to meet him. While I was there, his mother asked him for two dollars. He said he didn't have it, they passed words, and he walked out the door. When he was gone, his mother said, "Not for nothing, but I am happy he is going to jail." I just looked at her. I wasn't too sure of the situation, but I had suspected something was wrong with that family.

The morning my honeybun had to turn himself in, we woke up like usual except I went to work, and he went to jail. Before we parted, he just hugged me and kissed me and said he was sorry. I went to visit him every weekend for a month. During one visit Honey Buns mother was supposed to come with me and she didn't show up. When I walked in, he asked, "Where is my mother?" I said, "I don't know. Not here." He cried for the first forty minutes of the visit. I didn't know what to say, so I didn't say anything. He asked me to go to the block in his neighborhood where he used to be to meet someone and get money from them. While waiting, I stopped by to see his mother. At that time, we still did not know what the baby was. My honeybun's mother told me she hoped it would be a boy. As I was leaving, his mother said something only I heard: "Bitch."

So, I told her, "I am not a bitch." She said, "Yes, you are. You are my bitch." I told her I was not anybody's bitch. I told myself I would never go to her house again. I never have gone back to that lady's house—not in over eleven years. I really didn't deal with Honeybun's family much anyways. I only met his aunt after he went to jail. I had met his mother back in junior high school, of course. I have seen her since, but nothing serious happened.

The pregnancy became too much as far as my health. I had so much trouble moving around. I would twist my ankles often because my balance was so off. I started taking the bus because I gave my car back. I was paying $850 dollars a month for the car payment and the insurance. It was something I had been thinking about for a while. If I let go of my car, my kids could be in private school. So, I gave it up.

I held my baby shower in a community center that was a seven-dollar cab ride away from the area we lived in. Honeybun's mother saw somebody else I know and asked, "Did Alexis give you an *invitation* to the baby shower?" The girl said, "No, she just gave me the address." Honeybun's mother said, "The baby shower is far away. I don't know why she did the baby shower there. The time is so late, I don't think it's going to work out because people have got kids. I don't think I'm going." I think I told Honeybun that, but I don't remember. I had set the time of the baby shower from six to eleven o'clock p.m. because it was the only time the community center would give me— the rest was scheduled for a children's program or something. Honeybun called me from jail and said that his mother felt left out because I did not ask her to do anything for the shower. I told him there was nothing for her to do.

The aunt and her boyfriend helped me move around. They would pick me up from work, take me to eat, and everything. Also, on the day of the baby shower, they helped me set up. We had a lot to do decorating and picking up food. I was so tired.

Once the baby shower had started, Honeybun called his aunt's phone and told me his mother was getting dressed and she was coming. I said, "Why are you telling me that? I'll see her when she comes." He told me, "Fuck you." I hung up. The baby shower went on. Two people from my family came, the rest were friends and Honeybun's family. My son's grandmother and her family came. She always stood by me and supported me with everything and in every situation. Honeybun called back later that night on his aunt's phone. He asked me, "Is my mother there?" I said no. He said, "She didn't come?" I said nope. His parents did not show up—neither did my parents.

I continued going to work and to school. I was taking eighteen credits. When I went to my director's office at the case management job to tell her I was pregnant, I wound up telling her everything that was going on in my life just then. I cried in her office. She told me to take the rest of the day off and go home. I worked up until I was nine months pregnant. I had to stop working because my water started leaking out. I stopped working and going to school on November 29, 2007. I was able to hand in all my remaining work to the professors, so I would get my grades. Once I was home, I was finally able to relax.

The week of Christmas, my older sister and brother came knocking on the door. We talked, but not about the situation with the house. She invited me to go to Pennsylvania for Christmas, but my son (Ricardo) grandmother already invited me to go over to her house for Christmas.

Due to the fact I was home more now I had to go food shopping on a weekly basis. I remember praying to God, telling him I need a break and that I was tired. On December 30, 2007, at midnight, I started having labor pains. I was on the phone the whole time with my son's godmother. We timed the contractions, and once they were three minutes apart she came to take me to the hospital. I got to the hospital at four o'clock in the morning and had my daughter at 6:16 a.m. by way of natural birth. She weighed 6 pounds and 15 ounces.

My honeybun tried to call me, but I wasn't home I was still in the hospital. So, he called his mother to see if she knew where I was. She told him, "Congratulations, your baby is here." I never spoke to her to tell her I had the baby, but I did call his aunt, who must have told her.

Later on, my family came to see me and my baby girl. His grandmother, his aunt, and his little cousin came to see her. I named her Samia. My honeybun's mother did not even come see my daughter. My son's grandmother, by contrast, was there with balloons, flowers, and a teddy bear.

When my six weeks of maternity leave was up, I called my job to ask if they had a position available. My director told me no. I called the unemployment office the same day. I was okay with staying home with my kids. I had so much fun with them.

Shortly after that my health started to decline. I didn't understand why. My legs started to get weak, and my balance was still very off. My toes were numb. I went to the doctor, and they requested an MRI to test me for multiple sclerosis. My HMO kept rejecting the request for the test. It got so bad I could not even change the baby on my lap. My legs would be moving from side to side and my coordination was off.

I had been going to church with a friend from junior high school. She would come to pick me up every Sunday and help me to church. She would take Samia and me and sometimes Richie, my son. We went to church together for a couple of months. She helped me get to school as well. That was nice. I remember being in school, falling on the floor, falling outside, and even falling in the front of the school. I knew I had to get up and keep on going, though.

Honeybun's aunt helped me with the baby a lot. She also helped with my health by coming with me to the doctor and asking questions, making sure they did what they were supposed to do.

One day, his aunt asked me the next time Honey Bun called can you please add me to the call. She said she needed to talk to him. I did, but she didn't know I was still on the line during the phone call. She said, "Let me ask you a question. Do you want us to stop helping Alexis?" Honeybun said, "No. Why would you ask that?" She said, "Your mother said *you* said to stop helping her. To let her do stuff herself." He replied, "No! Help Alexis." I never said anything to him about it or let him know I heard the conversation.

I had asked Honeybun's aunt if she can ask if his little sister could come over to visit the baby. Honeybun mother said no, her daughter would meet my daughter when she comes up the block. His whole family lived in the same building, you see.

One time, I had to ask Honeybun's grandmother for eighty dollars for the baby—I don't remember why—but the grandmother sent Honeybun's brother to my house with the money. He had a hundred dollars. He was supposed to take twenty for himself and give me the other eighty for the baby. He only gave me thirty dollars and asked me if I was okay with that. I said yes. When Honeybun called, though, I told him that his brother took Samia's money. He didn't say anything. When I first gave birth to Samia, Honeybun's father came to my house at least five times a week to check on us, and he called every day to see if we needed anything. That was nice.

Honeybun eventually got released from prison. He came home, and one day after he had been out for a couple of months, I was outside with my cousin. I had Samia with me, and his mother walked right past the baby. Honeybun's little sister even said, "There's Samia." His mother looked at us, waved her hand, and walked into the store without stopping. I called and told Honeybun what had happened. He didn't say anything.

I saw his mother again a few days later, in front of her building. I was sitting there with her family. She walked right past everybody and did not speak to anyone. This was the second time she walked right past my daughter. That same day, later on, she came back out of the building, going to the store. By the time she came back from the store, Honeybun was there. He was standing behind Samia's stroller with his hands on the handle.

She bent down over the stroller to try and kiss Samia. The baby squeezed her lips away, so his mother moved off and just went in the building. I started crying. His family was staring at me. They said, "What happened? He was there." I said I couldn't deal with all this. I accepted that she did not want to deal with my daughter and would speak to her only when her father was around. What I am *not* going to do is allow her—or anyone—to confuse my baby.

I continued going to church during this time, and my health was still the same. We didn't know what was going on.

6 WHAT'S WRONG

I eventually went to a neurologist, who gave me a test to check and see if I had nerve damage. I took the test—no nerve damage. The MRI request had been rejected twice by this time.

After my appointment, I went back home. Honeybun was in the house with Samia. I told him the doctors said I might have MS. I asked him, "Are you going to leave me?" He said, "Hell no, Boo." He gave me a hug.

Once, I even dropped the baby. I was trying to walk to the bed, and I made it close and managed to put her on it before I fell, but I fell on the edge of the bed and that made her roll off the bed because of my weight pushing down on the edge of the mattress. I told my family what happened and that I needed help.

Honeybun's aunt, my friends, Richie's grandmother, my two younger boy cousins, and my cousin and her husband did what they could. One of my boy cousins would go to the store for me, food shop, whatever I needed him to do—still to this day he helps me. The other one he helped me for a little while till I got a home attendant. He went with me to the doctor, to get my hair done, to visit people. Around this same time, I had a situation where someone cashed in my food stamps and left me with only five dollars. I had saved fifty dollars on the card to get the baby more milk at the end of the month. I was with one of my girl cousins, so we called the card administrator phone line, and it told us when the money was taken off the card. My cousin was the only one who had my card the day the food stamps were used.

After that, Honeybun's aunt and her boyfriend took me everywhere I needed to go: WIC, doctor, shopping, church, and my friends' houses. His aunt stepped in and really became that mother figure to me. She went with me to appointments and asked questions. It was clear she was concerned.

Sometimes when we would go out to eat, people would ask if I was their daughter. We said yes. For my twenty-fifth birthday they bought me a pot set, and his great-grandmother gave me a card. My honeybun's aunt was in my house another day and they even slipped a check for the rent under the door. His aunt saw it and asked what it was for. I told her it was for the rent, but I hadn't paid it yet. She took the check home, paid the rent for me, and called me and told me it was taken care of. That was nice.

That summer, I thought about opening my own business: a preschool. I sat back and calculated the profit I could make, how many children I would take, the number of teachers, the cook, the furniture—everything. I asked my friend to be my business partner. I went to an office that helps minorities open businesses to talk to them about my idea.

Soon after that, Honeybun and I got into an argument we passed words. I said something about him and his mother being nobody. He said, "Well, least we got our high school diploma and GED." I said to him, "Okay, but what do either of you guys do with that education? I am going to get my GED *and* college degree." He said, "Sure, whenever *that* is."

When my daughter was eight months old, I found out I was pregnant again. I knew I could not keep the baby—I didn't want any more children just then. My honeybun wanted to keep the baby, but I decided to get an abortion. I took the abortion pill when I was six weeks along. I had to take one pill the same day I went to the clinic, then a day later I had to insert three pills in my vagina. I was gone for eight hours after I took the pills. I had both kids in the house on that day, and Honeybun was there too.

At this time, I was still in school, but I was taking independent study classes. I had four different professors. My laptop broke, and it was hard for me to get around to get to a computer to send in the work. I contacted one professor—a woman—to tell her I would send it on a certain day because I would have computer access. She said to me, "Why can't you just bring it in?" I told her my situation as far as my health went. I couldn't do it. She told me, "If you know you can't do this class, why are you still trying? The work is due." I told her I would continue to try until I got my degree because I wanted it. After I hung up with her, I started crying.

During this year, Honeybun's aunt did everything she could to get a home attendant for the kids and me. They denied my request for the services. It was okay, though, because Honeybun did everything: washed the clothes, cleaned up, food shopping, and went to get everything I needed.

A couple of months later, I had a fall in my apartment because I could not feel my legs. I had to go to the bathroom, but I wound up urinating on myself because I could not get up. I called

Honeybun and his aunt, and they came down the block. I took a shower and went to the hospital. My friend, my sister, and my honeybun's aunt went to the emergency room with me. I think my older brother was there as well, but I can't really remember.

They admitted me to the hospital for seven days to run tests and see what was going on. My gait was completely off. While I was in the hospital, they gave me four MRIs on my brain and full spine. Before they got the results, seven different doctors or so came in the room to see me. They asked me to pull my pants down and walk. I had to hold on to something to do it. They said at first it was due to a muscle I was supposed to have in my calf that everyone has, but because of the suspected MS they thought I didn't have it.

The next day, the head doctor came to my room and told me that my results came back. It was multiple sclerosis. I was just looking at the doctor, and I guess I had a strange smirk on my face. The doctor said, "It's not funny." I said I knew that. I sat there for like an hour, just staring at the wall and saying to myself, "I have MS. I have multiple sclerosis."

They sent me to check my eyes next, to see if the disease had affected them yet. They dilated my pupils to check the back of my eyes. I could not see for a few hours after that. Honeybun was there with me. The doctors were asking me what I could see while my eyes were dilated. I said, "I don't see anything." Honeybun said, "Alexis, stop saying you can't see." But I could not see *anything.* They started me on some medication and watched me to make sure the medicine agreed with my body.

My mother called me the day before I left the hospital. I told her I had MS. She said something was hurting her too, and that my sister fell, and "Now you with *this*?" We hung up. I called my cousin and told her what my mother had said. I cried.

Since I've been diagnosed I've only seen my mother five times in four years. The last time I saw my father I was twenty-one years old, and before that not since I was twelve years old.

I asked the doctor a lot of questions about MS. Can I give it to my kids? What are the medications for MS? Is there a cure? What do I need to do from this point on? The doctors told me I had "secondary progressive MS." She answered all the questions I asked her and told me as I aged it would get worse. The eventual outcome is you become blind and paralyzed. I prayed in the hospital and asked God to give me the strength to keep on going with my life. I asked him, "Please don't let any medication I take for the MS not agree with my body." I had to continue to move forward with my life. I had two children who did not ask to be here, and I had to take care of them. They didn't ask for me to give up on life and them just because I was going through something.

At my first visit with an MS specialist, she recommended that I start physical therapy to build up my leg strength and my upper-body strength. I got my request for a home attendant accepted right away too. The homemaker for the kids came months later. I had to move forward. God would never put more on you than you can bear.

At this point, I had eighty credits. I went right back to school that semester. The school was able to give me independent study classes again, like I had done the previous semester. I went to school and did physical therapy twice a week for eight months straight. I continued to fall from time to time. My balance was completely off still, but my legs got stronger. When I told my son, I was going back to school, he said, "Mom, how are you going to school with your legs?" I said to him, "I'm still here on earth, right? So okay, now it's time to finish school. In life, you get knocked down. But if you are determined, you can accomplish your goals."

I decided that I needed to take the next couple of years to try and figure out this disease. What was good for me, what's not? How the weather affects my health. What's a flare-up? What medication I could use when I am in remission or relapsing?

That February, I had a situation with my son's brother's mother. I had called his grandmother house, and the mother answered the phone. I asked if I could speak to Richie. She said, "Who? The father, or the son?" I said, "My son." She said something along the lines of, "You're just mad because I am his girl and I had his son." She meant my older son's father. I said, "You sound real dumb. You know if I wanted your man, I could have him." She said, "I don't care." I said, "Yes, you do." She said, "You crippled bitch." I said, "You know what? I'm not a broke bitch, you are a weave-wig-wearing twenty-eight-year-old phone operator. Bitch, you're too old to be answering phones. You need to stop chasing this nigger and go get a degree." She didn't say anything after that.

Richie's father called me later to find out what had happened exactly. He told me, "Your man needs to get you." I can't remember exactly what happened on the phone with him after that, but I hung up on him. My cousin called her later. I'm not sure what was said, but my cousin was at work so not much since she works in the hospital and is busy. My cousin told Richie's father baby mother to be ready, because there are a lot of people you have to go through to get to her.

My son and his grandmother were not there when all this happened—they were visiting someone in the hospital. I called his grandmother to let her know what was going on. By the time she and my son got back to the apartment, the girlfriend had people in the house ready to come to beat me up. My son had to see this.

A couple of months later, it was my son's birthday. I had wanted to take him out and sing "Happy Birthday" to him in a restaurant. I wanted to do this instead of having a party at home because I didn't want to be around his father or his girlfriend. Also, I did not want to put my son's grandmother in an awkward position. His grandmother decided to do cake and ice cream. His grandfather bought the cake for him. He wanted to just have the cake and ice cream at her house at first, and I had to tell him I didn't want to go to his grandmother's house because his father's girlfriend was likely to be there.

To find out for sure, I called his father and asked him if he was going to be there for the birthday celebration. He said he didn't know because the girl didn't want to go, and he didn't want to "hear my mouth." We hung up. I had to sit back and think. My son—any of my children—should never have to decide what parent could be there to sing "Happy Birthday" to them. That is selfishness.

I called the grandmother and told her they could come for cake. I could not see myself doing that to my son. He had the cake and ice cream. I didn't say anything to them, and they didn't say anything to me. My son had a party the following Saturday at Chuck E. Cheese's, and they were both invited. It was cool; he was there with her and their kids. I was there with my family. I saw that it was bothering my son that he did not see his father anymore, not since he moved in with his girlfriend.

My aunt had started coming over to help me with whatever I needed help with—cleaning or cooking or taking my daughter outside for a little while. We helped each other in a pinch. One day, I was on my way to church with the homemaker and home attendant. I had Samia with me. I saw a lady who had known me from the time I was a baby. She asked me if Samia was related to Honeybun's aunt. I said yes, and she said, "Let me tell you one thing: you deserve so much better. From what I know about Honeybun, he deals with a lot of girls. I will talk to you later, when you are alone." I suggested we sit down and talk on the bench right then.

I asked everyone else to walk ahead and give me a second. She said for a couple of months, Honeybun's mother had been talking about some girl, calling the girl a "project bitch." His mother said "That bitch is going around saying my son is the father of her baby. That is *not* his child." She was calling *me* all kinds of dumb bitches, saying her son could have anybody he wants, so why settle for *her*? Meaning me. The mother said, "She needs to find her baby father."

When the lady found out it was me that Honeybun's mother was talking about, she told Honeybun's mother, "You need to be proud that your son is with a girl like that. She has an education, a work history. She doesn't do what these girls be doing out here. She's sick and is still a good mother. That same little girl you're not claiming—you are going to need her, and if Karma didn't hit you yet it's coming. You ought to be ashamed of yourself."

7 LIVING LIFE

After she had told me all that, I left and went to church. After the service was over, I went to use the bathroom. When I came out, someone asked me what was wrong, and I started crying. I wasn't crying because of what his mother said. I know I don't do half the stuff people could do, but I was the topic of everybody's discussions, and I was tired of it. I spoke with an elder from church, then I went home.

I decided to sit in the park in front of my building with Samia. I saw Honeybun. He could tell I was crying, so he asked me what happened. I told him his mother was talking about me. He asked me who told you that, but I said it wasn't important and if the information wasn't sufficient, I would not be crying. He said, "Since you don't want to tell me who said it, I do not want to hear it." Then he walked away.

I went in the house and packed his stuff. He had to leave. It was too many situations with his mother and if he couldn't say anything to her, if he wouldn't defend my daughter and me to his family, who would? I knew it would get out of control if I said anything to them. He came back later on to find the door locked. I lived on the first floor, so he went around to the window and opened it. He asked, "Alexis? What happened?" I said, "It's too much. I'm tired of you and your mother. I don't need this."

He called his mother to find out if it was true. I don't think she knew the phone was on speaker. She told him, "Just because she wants to start up with her bullshit—don't put me in that." I said, "What bullshit?" I told her she was ignorant and needed to grow up. She said, "You need to grow up." I said, "If you haven't noticed, I have. Why do you think I've been ignoring you all this time?" I told Honeybun, "I can't even walk and hold my kid's hand. You think I have time to sit here and make up lies about your mother?" He was looking at me. He said no. He would not leave me alone with all this.

They cut my Medicaid off, which meant I did not have any medication or any more physical therapy. I wasn't worried, because I trust in God. He might not be there when you want, but He is always on time. I went to a Fourth of July cookout in Pennsylvania with my children, Honeybun's aunt, and her boyfriend. Some of my family member were there. We were talking about my health, and I told my aunt my Medicaid was cut off and I wasn't doing physical therapy or taking medication since it cost $3,600 a month out of pocket. She told me to find out how much the physical therapy would be and to let her know.

On my way home, I called Richie's grandmother to let her know I didn't think I could drop Richie off because Honeybun's aunt's boyfriend had to go to work. When I got home, I called Richie's grandmother again. His father's girlfriend picked up. I asked if I could speak to Richie's grandmother. She told me to hold on and then *click!* I hung up. Richie's father called my house saying, "You a dumb bitch. Don't disrespect my girl." He cursed me out, calling me all kinds of bitches. I started crying and asked him what he was talking about. He said *I* said something to his girl when I called. I hung up. I was crying not because of anything he said over the phone in particular, but everything that was going on in my life at that time. My son called his father and said, "Why are you calling here, disrespecting my mother? She didn't even do anything." His father told him, "Watch it. When I see you, I am going to hit you." My son replied that next time he saw his little half-brother, he was going to punch him in the face. My son was nine years old.

My son came in the room and asked if I was okay. I told him I was fine and not to worry about me. We started talking, and he told me he went to Yogi Bear Sunday School and they asked anyone who had a situation to pray about to come up to the front. He said, "Mom, I prayed for three things. You want to know what? For the kids to stop bullying me in school, for my mother to get better, and for my father to love me." I wanted to cry, but I couldn't do it in front of him. I cried later. I didn't want him to feel like he shouldn't tell me stuff because it might make me cry. My poor baby. I asked my son how he felt about his father, and he said he didn't like him. I said, "Not because of me, right?" He said, "No. He doesn't love me. Mom, I feel like I have to protect you and my sister. He's treating you this way and you're disabled. It's not right."

About that time, there was a family reunion. Something was telling me not to go, but I went anyway. My son's grandmother came with her mother and sisters. Honeybun's family came, including his aunt, his great-grandmother, and his cousins. I was sitting at a table at first, but then my legs started getting stiff, so I laid down on I blanket. My cousin and my uncle started fighting. I don't know why—I was in my own world just thinking about walking like everyone else was doing, holding their kids, not fighting.

I was sitting there talking to one cousin, and my other cousin came over. So, my cousin who was sitting there first asked what happened—I guess with the fight. My other cousin said, "I already know what you're going to say. He runs to your house, telling you all these sob stories." I said, "What are you talking about? I didn't even say anything about the fight." She kept talking, and I told her to leave me alone, but she wouldn't. I don't even know what she said. Finally, I told her to get out of my face. She said, "Who the fuck do you think you're talking to?" She moved closer to my face and said, "Get up and *move* me out. Who the fuck do you think you're talking to? I'm not your kids. Get up and move me!" I started crying, and my other cousin started crying too.

I was sitting there on the blanket, crying and dizzy. They got me some water. I found out the next day talking to another cousin who was there exactly what she had been saying; I did not hear any of that. I was in another world.

I went to Pennsylvania for my mother's birthday—and to get away from Honeybun and the things he was doing at the time. I can't remember exactly when this situation happened, but we'd had an argument. I told him I was a damn good mother in this predicament or out of it. He said, "I know I lot of good mothers." I said, "Name one." He didn't have anything to say.

Two months later, my cousin called me—
the one I had an argument with at the family
reunion. She asked if she could come to my house. I
said sure. She came, but we did not talk about the
situation.

My younger sister had also moved in with
me from Pennsylvania about that time. Then I found
out that I was pregnant again. This time, I decided
to keep the baby. I told my MS doctor that I was
pregnant, and she said "Great." I had to stop taking
my medication. I didn't tell anybody right away; the
idea of having another baby had to grow on me.
Honeybun knew, and a couple of friends. I had
decided to go to a high-risk pregnancy clinic to
make sure the baby was okay, but the doctors told
me my illness couldn't do anything to the baby.
This meant I had to go to the doctor more than the

normal, though. My friend came with me to my first appointment.

By the time I was four months along, everyone knew. I remember being in the house with my daughter—she was nineteen months old. I had made some food for dinner, and I went into the kitchen to plate it up, but I was struggling. Samia was watching me. I came out of the kitchen and was walking into the other room when I dropped the plate of food on the floor. I went and sat on the couch because I knew I was going to fall. My daughter went over to where the food fell on the floor. She put the plate in her doll baby's stroller, picked the food up and put it on the plate, and rolled her baby stroller over to me. I wanted to cry. I had just been thinking to myself, "How am I going pick this food up?" But she did it by herself. She looked at me like, "Mommy, don't worry. I got it." How could I cry? This little person was put here for a reason. Thank you, God.

My little sister was away in Pennsylvania visiting my mother and siblings. She had been accepted to Long Island University studying premed—she wanted to become a surgeon. I had put in for a transfer to a bigger apartment because I had a one-bedroom and we needed more space.

8 LIFE WITH M.S

I continued on with my schooling at the College of New Rochelle. I had 109 credits—I only needed 11 more to graduate. I took the next semester off because I was pregnant, and the baby's due date was around the time of finals. I didn't want to take that chance. So, I took off a semester to welcome my baby.

Within a month of putting in the request for a bigger apartment, they called me back about a four-room apartment. This was in December 2009. By January 2010, I had moved into my new apartment. I was still pregnant.

Samia's second birthday came. It fell on a weekday, so we cooked on that day and got her a cake, then we threw her a party in Chuck E.

Cheese's on the following Saturday. I didn't invite too many people, but everyone came except Honeybun's mother. I never asked ever what happened.

While pregnant, I fell a couple of times—but not on my stomach. One night I went to the bathroom, but I fell and hit my head on the wall. I tried to get up but couldn't, I was so dizzy. My little sister was on the phone with my older sister trying to figure out a way to help me up. We called Honeybun too, but he did not answer. So, we called my aunt's house. My uncle was there, and he came down the block to help me. I was living two blocks away from my grandmother and a block away from my aunt. Being pregnant with MS was very tricky and risky, so I was glad to have family nearby.

Around this time, I remember Honeybun

being sick. He had come over. I had company, and he called me in the next room and said, "Alexis, call my mother." I said, "Call your mother for *what*?" He said, "You need to stop acting like that. Just call her."

I called her to make him happy. She said, "Honeybun shouldn't be around you when he's sick and you're pregnant. If you get sick, you can't take any medication." I was quiet the whole conversation. She finished talking, I said "Okay," and we hung up. I knew that Honeybun did not really believe me about the things his mother had done to me.

Honeybun and I started passing words. I said, "You run your mouth when you shouldn't, but when you should your mouth stays closed." He said, "You do not know what you're talking about." I said, "Everything your mother says about us… you never say anything! Whatever I told you, you didn't believe."

A friend I used to work with had the same name as me. She called me about this same time because a girl had left a message on her phone about Honeybun. She said she heard that I was pregnant—and she was too. This was in March.

My honeybun went out, then came back drunk and went to the wrong floor. He was knocking on someone else's door, but they did not answer. He fell asleep in front of the wrong person's door. They woke him up, and he came up to my apartment and knocked on the door. It was locked, and when no one answered he kicked the door till it opened. I asked my cousin to call his mother to see if her boyfriend could come and get

Honeybun and his stuff. She called his mother, who told her boyfriend "I'm sick of this shit. He needs to get all his shit out of that house and leave." My cousin did not tell me this right away, as it was my baby shower week. Between this and the voice mail message, I wanted him out. So, when Honeybun kicked the door down, I called the cops.

I had my baby shower for my youngest son, and it was nice. Some friends came, and a little bit of my family. His aunt came, his great-grandmother, his father, and his uncle—but his mother was not allowed. It was a small shower, nothing big. My honeybun never had a baby shower.

I went to the doctor for a nine-month prenatal checkup to make sure the baby was healthy and ready to enter the world swinging. I left my two-year-old daughter, Samia, in the house with the homemaker. When I left, I got in my wheelchair. Samia was crying and reaching her hands out for me to pick her up. I had called the house several times to check up on Samia to make sure she was okay while I was gone. After the appointment, I called because I had to go to get the baby some Pampers really quick from a store near the hospital. I wanted to let the homemaker know and to see how my baby was doing.

When I got home, I found my daughter asleep in her bed. She woke up and the homemaker brought her to me. She had a burn on her arm to the white meat. When I saw it, my mouth dropped open? I asked the homemaker how it happened. The homemaker stated, "I don't know. She was fine when I put her down for her nap." I took a picture of the burn and sent it to her dad, who had seen her that morning. He went to the pharmacy and bought bacitracin ointment, gauze, tape, and cream—all kinds of stuff to put on the burn.

He called his mother to ask what to do, and she told him, "Don't take Samia to the doctor. Just put the stuff on it and wrap it up." I said, "Who does she think she is talking to? I am calling the doctor!" I called her PCP, Dr. Chadda, and informed her about the situation. She said, "Please bring her in if the burn is that severe." I got my baby dressed, and we went to the clinic. I'd be damned if I wasn't taking my child to the doctor when she had clearly suffered a burn like that. The doctor examined her and said it was a first-degree burn. The same doctor had seen my daughter two time just two weeks before the burn: once for a checkup and the second for a flu shot. So, she knew what condition my daughter's health was in normally. She gave her cream, gauzes, tape, and bacitracin. She told me to clean the wound three times a day. I went out and brought her an aloe plant too and put that on it when I cleaned the burn. It healed good and fast. Thank God I took her to the clinic, because on my way back into the house ACS was waiting to come in the door with me. I had to take her back the next week to see the doctor, so she could see her burn. She said it was healing well. I blamed myself for my daughter getting burned, and I did not speak to anyone for about a month. Really—I didn't have a conversation with anyone.

ACS came back the very next morning and asked to speak to me, Honeybun, and the home attendant in separate rooms, one right after another.

I had to wait two months for Albany to make the decision about whose fault it was. The homemaker stayed in my house for two days after the burn happened, but I asked for her to be taken off the case. When I asked her what had happened, she said she didn't know, she just saw her scalded arm. I said, "I called four times! When were you going to tell me.?" Something happened to my baby while I wasn't home, but the homemaker was in the house with my daughter. And she claimed she did not know what happened. The homemaker had to go.

When I fell in the bathroom hit my head, it scared me. I decided when I was around eight months pregnant to get a wheelchair, so I wouldn't fall on my stomach while trying to walk. I was ready gave birth to my baby.

I went to a regular a checkup appointment.

When I got there, the doctors checked me and said I was three centimeters dilated. They didn't want to send me home, so they told me to sit in the waiting room for one hour to see if I dilated some more. When I went back in the exam room, they saw I had dilated another half a centimeter. You have to be four centimeters to be admitted to the hospital when you're having a baby. So, I left and went home. I couldn't do that much walking, so I just relaxed. By eleven o'clock that night, the contractions started coming. I called Honeybun's aunt—Honeybun was already in the house. We left and went to the hospital. We got there at two o'clock. The nurses triaged me immediately and hooked up the baby monitor to my stomach. By the time they moved me to a room, my water had broken. I asked the doctor if I could get pain medication. She checked me and said I was ready to deliver my son. He came into this world at 3:36am weighing 7 pounds, 7 ounces, and measuring 19 inches. A natural birth again! I named him Jason.

I stayed in the hospital for three days. The baby stayed in the room with me. My health was the same—my balance was still off, and I couldn't walk alone. One of the nurses came in the hospital room and asked me why I keep having kids if I know I can't take care of them. I said I didn't know and I started crying. I told my friend what happened. She was upset, but I told her it was okay.

About two weeks after I got home, a girl called my house and said, "You stupid bitch. I am going have ACS at your door and a dick waiting to be put in Samia's mouth. Fuck that little bastard in your stomach." It was the same girl who had left a message in March—I recognized the voice. I called my aunt to let her know of the situation just in case something happened so someone else would know what was going on.

A few weeks passed, and then it was Father's Day. My honeybun had told me that he was going to an all-white party that night. I had woken up at about five in the morning, and something told me to call his phone. That same girl answered. She said, "I can't hear you. Let me call from my house phone." She called back, and I let her talk. She said Honeybun was her man, and that they had been in a relationship for eight years. She also told me that my honeybun said he told her it wasn't anything serious with me, he was just my daughter's father. I asked her, "Didn't he tell you he just had a son with me, who is two months old? He signed the birth certificate with his whole name. He was there for the labor. He was there throughout my whole pregnancy. She said, "No. I'm ecstatic right know because I did not know nothing about your baby." She went on to say, "I cheated on Honeybun and had a daughter with some else. When you had your daughter, he had a daughter on me. I know what your daughter got for Christmas—I was with him. We were shopping for my daughter's stuff and I had to force him to buy Samia gifts." She did tell me accurately some of the stuff my daughter got for Christmas that year.

I asked her why they didn't have kids eight years ago, then. She said he wasn't ready to be a dad. She also stated that Honeybun and his father took her out for Mother's Day. She said, "I'm going ask him some questions about your son." She put the phone down, and I could hear her ask him to go home to Alexis's house, and told him he couldn't stay at her house. She said she asked him the same question a couple of times, then he said, "I don't know what you're talking about." She said, "Honeybun, do you have a son with Alexis? Were you there for the birth?" He said, "No, I wasn't there."

I guess at that point he got up and went to the bathroom. I could hear footsteps over the phone. I think she followed him to the bathroom. She said to him, "Let me come in." He said, "No. I'm going to the bathroom. Move out of my way." She said, "My mother wants to talk to you and say, 'Happy Father's Day.'" She put the phone to his ear and said, "Talk, Mom." I said, "Good morning, Honeybun. I heard everything you said about my son not being yours." Then I heard the girl in the background saying, "He's up now!"

When I got off the phone with the girl, I was thinking to myself "This girl is crazy". Did she forget she called my friend's phone in March, saying she heard I was pregnant? Saying ACS is going be at my door and she's going to have a dick waiting to put in Samia's mouth and fuck that little bastard in my stomach? She's bugged out. She really did *not* know about my son. Crazy. Eight years is a long time to be with someone to know if you want to grow with them, but he says he wasn't ready for children and still took care of your daughter."

He left her house and came to my house. By the time he got to my apartment, all his stuff was packed. I called the cops and told him to get out.

They just told him to go for a walk.

A couple of weeks later, my son had a doctor's appointment. I told Honeybun to come so we could do the DNA test. He said, "I'm not taking a test. I know that's my son." I said, "That's not what you said." He said, "She never asked me that. You don't understand." I said, "I understand what I heard. You denied he was your son." He said, "No, I would never deny my kids being mine. She was lying." We never took the test.

By that point, I was thinking about going into a nursing home to get better intensive therapy to strengthen my legs. I would have to leave for thirty days. I couldn't leave my kids for that long, though. I called two of my friends to see if they would keep the kids for me for a month. They both said yes. I wanted to get better for my children, but

I knew I had to figure out another alternative because leaving my kids with my friends for so long was not an option.

I decided to go in the hospital for a few days and take steroids instead. I was admitted for four days and was given a thousand milligrams a day of steroids. They also gave me prednisone to take for six weeks after being released. The medication made me gain weight, and my face swelled from it. It fixed some things with my balance, but not everything. I was sitting in my room one night, rocking the baby to sleep when I realized that was something I could never have done before I went into the hospital. I started crying, thanking God, and saying to myself, "I knew it wasn't going to be like this forever." I realized I had also been able to sit up for long periods of time and hold the baby for longer than usual.

I got up after I finished rocking the baby, got out of the bed, and started rocking from side to side, saying to myself, "I knew it." During the six weeks I was on the steroid, I was able to get up in the morning and cook breakfast, lunch, and dinner. I even went downstairs to meet my cousin by myself with just the walker. I was happy. It was a great feeling to be able to do those things. The only bad side effect was the swelling.

9 CHASING A DREAM

At the end of August, I was home with the kids, my little sister, and Honeybun. The captain of NYPD knocked on my door. Honeybun knew they were looking for him, so he got in the closet. The captain asked me if I had seen Honeybun and told me he had kidnapped his girlfriend and abducted her. I said, "No, I have not seen him for a couple months now." I also told them I had called his probation officer to tell them he didn't live with me and to take my address off his case file—but that's how the cops got my address. The captain asked me if he could search the apartment to make sure Honeybun was not there. I said yes even though I knew he was in the closet. The cops found him and arrested him. While he was walking out in handcuffs he was trying to talk to me, but I never looked at him. He called when he got to the precinct, but I hung up when I heard his voice.

I got a phone call one night at four o'clock in the morning. In hindsight, I'm not sure if it happened before the cops came to my door or after. It was a different girl asking Honeybun a question she procced to say, "You good?" In the background you can hear him say "Yeah, I'm good. You good?" then she hung up. So, I called her number back from my cell phone. She didn't pick up the first time. So, I called a second time, and she picked up and hung up. I called again and left a message saying, "I'm not sure why you're calling me, but if it was me calling you, I would let you hear something you could never get over. Don't call me anymore."

I woke up that morning and changed my

house number. I changed the slider on my lock. I wanted him to go. I was dealing with enough.

The girl had called my cell phone back, and when I picked up, she had already hung up. She called back and said, "Are you and Honeybun together?" Then she hung up again. I never called back. She called back and said, "Why won't you let Honeybun see his kids?" I picked up on the fact that she *wanted* me to call her phone. Turns out she had an order of protection against Honeybun. Honeybun called me and said, "My probation officer just called and said stop answering the phone if it's that girl. She called my probation officer and told him you are harassing her by calling her phone. If she calls your phone, do not answer. If it's a private number don't pick up. If you do pick up and hear her voice, hang up." He told me what happened

139

between them—something with money, I don't know.

A few weeks later the girl called my phone again and said, "I couldn't talk to you before because he was in my face." She asked what he was telling me about her. I said, "That's your boyfriend?" She said yes. I said, "He told me it's nothing, just business." She started crying, so I asked her why. She said, "Who the fuck does he think he is? That motherfucker's gonna go to jail." I also told her he said we should change our number, and then she started crying more. I asked her if she had an order of protection against Honeybun, and she said yes. She said, "I'm walking to the precinct right now. He said he's going to take my daughter out of school." I said, "So he's around your kids often?" She said no. She asked me when the last time, I slept with him. I said, "This morning, before he left." She was just crying and crying, but she also said, "So he argues with you and comes right to me." I said to her, "What makes you think he argues with me?" That was that. I changed my number.

I had gone back to school to get those last eleven credits to graduate, and I didn't have time to deal with bullshit. I had decided to split the remaining credits up. I would have to take six this semester and five the next semester. I also had to take independent study classes online.

I remember one Friday morning. It was 8:00 in the morning, and I had gotten up to go to the bathroom. The kids were home with me. When I got up, though, I fell on the floor. With MS, if you have to use the bathroom, you can't hold it for a long time. Some people with MS even have to use a catheter bag. I could not make it. So, I had to urinate in my son's Pampers. Then I scooted myself across the floor to the bathroom and lifted myself up with the tub and the sink. I told my daughter to stay on the bed with the baby. She was only two and a half years old then, and my son was three months. She tried to feed the baby while I was in the bathroom and spilled all the milk all over the bed. By the time I got up and managed to walk back into the bedroom, it was 8:45am. I was so tired. Things like this happen all the time with MS. I thank God the kids were okay.

One day, I gone out somewhere and left the homemaker in the house with the kids, but she needed to leave. I needed someone to go to the house to sit with the kids until I could get there. Honeybun called his mother, and she came down the block. When I got home, she was there. She talked to me for a few minutes, then asked me to loan her twenty dollars until she got her money. I gave it to her.

The next morning, I left to go to Pennsylvania for Thanksgiving. From the beginning, I did not want to go. But I went up there with the kids. We cooked dinner at my sister's house, then went over to my aunt's house to eat. There were six of us sitting at the table eating, and the topic came up of whether you would know if your kid was smoking or drinking. My older sister said you *would* know if your kid is smoking or drinking because they crave the drug. She said something else too, but I don't remember exactly what. I told her I *didn't* think you would be able to tell if your child was using drugs. Your child could be high and drunk the whole time they are not around you and sober up before they come home. OR put Visine in their eyes. How would you know what they do when they are with their friends? She said, "So what are you saying? I don't know what I am talking about?" I said, "This is part of having a conversation. Everyone is entitled to their own opinion. If I offended you in any way, I am sorry. Having a conversation is like a debate—you agree to disagree." She told me, "You don't know what you're talking about. It doesn't matter. Let me get the fuck out of here." She got up from the table and went in the living room to play cards. I stayed at the dining room table, doing my crossword puzzle and listening to my iPod. I said to myself, "Maybe I should go home to avoid problems." Honeybun called me, but I did not tell him what was going on with my sister and me. Honeybun's car was too small to take all three kids, the dog, my bags, and my walker anyway. So, I had to text one of my uncles and ask him if could come and pick me up. He said he couldn't because he did not have his car. I asked him for my other uncle's number, and he gave it to me. I called *him* and asked him if he could come get me, but he said he couldn't.

One of my uncles was there at my aunt's house, but I didn't ask him because I did not know he was ready to leave. While I was sitting in the dining room, my cousin came in and asked me if I wanted to go into the living room. She was trying to help me, but I said no. I was crying. I wanted to go home. So, my uncle came in the dining room and said, "Alexis, you should've told me you wanted to leave."

My sister told my uncle that if we planned to get our stuff from her house that we had to go now because she was leaving. From where I was sitting at my aunt's dining room table I could see my sister—she was moving her head and everything. I said to her, "All that is uncalled for." She said, "I am not talking to you." I said, "You're talking *about* me." She said, "You need to have respect— I'm your older sister." I said to her, "Do you even know what it means to have respect for someone? I'm tired of you. Every fucked-up thing you did to me, I walked away from. I'm tired of you. I don't need this. Who *are* you?" I was still crying. She was talking the whole time I was saying this. She told my older son if it wasn't for her we wouldn't have anything, but I don't know what else she said. I only heard what she said at the beginning of the argument. I was still sitting at the dining room table the whole time we were passing words.

Honeybun had my keys to the house, so I couldn't leave until I got in contact with him. My oldest son suddenly started crying. I asked him why and he said because he did not want to go to my sister's house, he wanted to go home. My uncle pulled him to the side to talk to him. I went back to my sister's house and we stayed there till the morning, when my uncle said we could leave.

When I woke up that morning, I stayed in the bed with the baby. My niece came in the room two times to ask me if I wanted to eat. I told her no because I didn't want to eat food in her house. My uncle called me at about 1:00 p.m. to tell me to get ready, because he was coming. So, I started packing. My older sister got up and got in her car—

she wanted to go shopping since it was Black Friday. My little sister started helping me pack, but when she found out my older sister was going shopping she left with her. I was in the house with my brothers and my mother. My mother left as well, saying she had to go pick her boyfriend up from the bus station to take him home and then she was going to work. My seven-year-old niece helped me pack and get ready. She had to help me get in the tub to wash up, and she stood beside me passing me everything I needed to get dressed. She had to sit on the bags to close them and put bacon bites in the dog bag to get the dog to go in—all while she was holding the baby. Even If I wanted to cry, I couldn't. My uncle came, and we left.

On our way back, I had called Honeybun's mother to ask her to call him, so I could get my key.

She said she would, and I called my two friends to meet me in front of my building to help me get settled in because no one was there. We made it home, and Honeybun and my friends were there waiting in front of the building. They helped me unpack and feed the kids. Toward the end of the night, I started to feel sick. When I don't feel well, my arms and legs are weak, and my head sometimes hurts. When that happens, I can't hold the baby to feed him or do anything—I'm too weak. So, one of my friends called Honeybun's aunt and told her they didn't know what was going on, but when honeybuns aunt called me to ask what happened I told her to ask Honeybun about the situation, and was there someone who would pick his stuff up? She said" I don't have anyone to pick up his stuff."

his grandmother called, and she told my

friend that I needed to leave Honeybun alone. She told her this was not the first time this had happened and that I just acted this way when I didn't get my way with him. No one spoke to his mother, but she called my cell phone and said to my other friend, "Alexis acts this way when she doesn't get her way with Honeybun, but when things are going her way, she is all lovey-dovey with him." My friend hung up on her. One of my friends left, and the other one spent the night with us. The next day when I got up, I called the aunt and told her to tell her sister and her nieces to never call my phone again and to tell Honeybun's mother to give me back the money I had loaned her. I had had enough with this situation with his mother.

At this point, I told Honeybun we needed a break. my son was four months old, and my daughter was two and a half years old. I couldn't

do this anymore.

10 JUST KEEP LIVING LIFE

I called my aunt and I told her the situation. She told me, "I'm going to take care of it." I told her not to say anything to Honeybun's mother because she was not worth it. My aunt came to visit me the next day at my house. I told her the story and that his mother owed me money. My aunt said she was going up to her house. I told my aunt when she got the money back from his mother, she should keep it—I didn't even want the money. Since his mother wanted to run her mouth, I wanted her to have to pay it back. My aunt saw his mother and told her that she needed to stay out of my relationship with her son. My aunt told her that I had to deal with enough every day, and that everything she was doing by bringing the drama was something her niece didn't need. They discussed the money, and she paid it back to my aunt. I had spoken to my kids' godmother on the phone and told her everything that was going on. She said, "Girl, God's got something good in store for you."

The next month, it was Christmas—and Samia's birthday. Honeybun's aunt and the rest of the family members who had bought my kids a gift sent them down the block, so the kids could have the gifts on Christmas Day. Honeybun came to my house, and we were sitting in the living room opening the gifts with the kids. He asked me to get Samia dressed because he wanted to take her up the block to see his family. I told him she wasn't going anywhere, and that everybody from up that block that got her a gift had already sent it down. I asked him why his mother couldn't have just sent her gifts along too. He said, "Why can't my kids go see my family?" I said, "Do you not see what is going on? Your mother only asks to see the kids only one day out of the year. She is trying to be funny. Last year I let her go, but this year... no." He went and got the gifts from his mother and brought them to the kids.

That next week, it was Samia birthday. I gave her a party. On the day of her birthday, we cooked a dinner and got her a cake and balloons. Honeybun knew the party started at four o'clock, but her father didn't get to the party until 4:00 p.m. The party was on January first, but the night before when the ball dropped he did not even call his kids to say, "Happy New Year's."

There were two private number missed calls on my phone. Two girls that I knew came to Samia's party, and they told me they had seen him at the club with a few guys and a girl. My close friend had gone up to him and said, "I know you're not trying to play my friend." The girl was apparently standing right there when she said this. He told my friend, "Hell no." When he got to the party, I told him, "You were at a club with people, but you couldn't call your kids last night?" That was my only issue—it made me mad he wouldn't acknowledge my kids. Forget him and the girl, I thought. I had bigger problems.

Sometime Later on, somebody said they saw him washing clothes with the girl, but I don't know this person—it was a friend of someone I know.

I had started my last semester of school. I was taking statistics for the second time, because I failed it the first time. I was also sending letters out to several famous people regarding my book and a paper I wrote in class the previous semester.

Two months later, someone I know saw him in Target with a girl—and a little girl. I knew he had also cut his hair. When the person called and told me, I didn't say anything. she mentioned his haircut, which I never told her, so this was it. It was him. He had some things of mine, so I had to call his father to tell him to just bring me my stuff.

Honeybun called. I never asked about the situation. He was mad, but at this point I really didn't care. When I had asked him in the past about the girls, he had always said everything was just business. I told him he needed to go and get himself together. What good is he to me and my children if he is not good to himself? I told him take as much time as he needed. I also told him I didn't know if I would be there when he came back. This had to be in August of 2010, and my baby was four months old. I couldn't do it anymore. I had bigger problems.

I continued to take care of myself and my children, and to send out my letters regarding my book and school. I'm not too good in math, so to pass statistics I had to take my mind off all the unimportant stuff and focus. My son turned one on April 27, 2011. I took him to get pictures and we got him a cake, cooked dinner, and sang "Happy Birthday." His dad was there, and my aunt. It was fine.

The following Monday was my birthday. I turned twenty-eight, and my close friend came over with a cake and balloons. I didn't do anything special that day—I was just grateful to see twenty-eight years old.

That Wednesday was the final exam for my math class, so on my birthday Monday and Tuesday I was studying. I went to take the test for my GED and the completion of college. I passed and was done! Being that I took statistics again late, my GED needed to be on file before my degree could be issued. I would have to walk in the graduation ceremony the following year, but I would get my degree in August and my GED in six weeks. I also started working on my next plan: opening a shelter for homeless teens. I was also planning to enroll in the Credentialed Alcoholism and Substance Abuse Counselor (CASAC) program and starting a master's program in two years.

The two younger kids' dad called me saying he needed to talk. I said, "I am listening." He said, "I am ready to leave the streets alone. Are you ready to get married? I am ready to get married. I want my family."

I told him I would call him back. I didn't know if I wanted to be married. I never called him back about that situation.

In September of 2011, a new homemaker started working with us, and a new home attendant as well. The homemaker was there for about a month when I realized she was stealing from me. Every day I would check my kitchen cabinets after she would leave for her shift. She also would come in and cook herself something quick to eat but was not feeding my kids. It was bad. My baby came to me and said, "Mommy, she hit me." I called her and asked her about it. She said, "You know I did not hit him." But I knew that was a lie and I needed proof. It had been going on for about two or three months. I wanted to catch her on camera so I could send it to the news. I brought in a nanny camera to monitor the situation. It was not okay to do this to someone disabled. I wasn't able to catch her because the camera started to freeze or glitch and on the final day, she was in my home she left with a hundred dollars—and the camera. I found out through the agency that she and the home attendant were in it together. That's how she knew to walk out with the camera. Everything she took honeybun replaced.

In January of 2012, I went to get an MRI on my brain and spine to check the progression of my MS. The specialist showed the areas were the disease was shrinking. She said, "I don't know what you are doing, but keep doing it!"

On graduation day, I was super excited. I

finally made it! I took Access-A-Ride to get there. Driving downtown, I felt like crying because I was going by myself. I told myself, "Don't cry. You've waited for this day for six years. It means a better life for you and your children." After the graduation, I was really surprised to see that my uncle had come to the ceremony. I did not see him during the graduation, though, because he was up on the balcony in Radio City Music Hall. At the ceremony, seeing families there with flowers, I said to myself that I wish I had flowers. After the ceremony was over, my uncle came downstairs. He had flowers and a teddy bear. I wanted to cry.

In August 2012, I was going to exchange clothes at a store when I ran into my kids' grandmother (Honeybun's mother). She was with her daughter, talking to her mother-in-law. I went

THE WAR BEHIND MY SMILE

over there and hugged the little sister and said, "Hi! How are you?" The mother said hello to me, but I ignored her. She said, "I am saying hi to you." This was on a Thursday, but I had also seen her the previous Monday and she did not speak to me then. So, I wasn't speaking to her now. I ignored her. She said, "Don't be mad at me because my son doesn't want you." I looked at her and wanted to say, "No, your son doesn't know what to do with *this* woman because he did not get that love from *you*. So, he doesn't know how to treat and love a woman". Then she said to me, "It's good for you that you are in a wheelchair." She was *happy* I couldn't walk. I looked at her and said, "Bye, crackhead." Then I moved away.

While getting in the car, my aunt came walking around the corner asking what the fuck just had happened. I said it was nothing, and we left.

Something told me to call my aunt later. I did, and she told me she went to Honeybun's mother's house and the kids' dad's girlfriend opened the mother's door. His mother came to the door and my aunt said she slapped the shit out of her. She told her, "Nobody better call or go to my niece's house. Next time, I am going to break your ass in half." Then she walked away. The kids' dad's girlfriend was walking behind my aunt asking, "What happened? What happened?" My aunt told her, "Bitch, if you don't get away from me, I am going to slap the shit out of you too." She walked away.

I never heard anything from his mother again.

This was the year I became a full-time single parent of three children. My oldest son's grandparents never gave me a chance to ask for anything for my son, though. They just bought things for him. They made good on the promise they made me when I was pregnant: "You have this baby. My wife and I will take care of this baby. You and my son take care of yourselves." They lived up to it. My son is now eighteen years old, and they've helped me all this time.

As for my two younger children, I would never bring them in this world not being able to provide for them and myself financially. They also have an amazing grandfather who is there when or if I need him.

In 2013, I requested a new homemaker to assist me with my kids. She was around my age. She was with us for a year, but then I eventually took her off the case because she was talking about my personal business to other people. There was

nothing to tell me and the kid's father were not

together, and it's not her place to share my business.

She knew that I was aware of her telling my

business to other people. The last straw was when

my son had a doctor's appointment, but the weather

was so bad I couldn't go. She also did not come to

work that day. This was her second day of not

showing up to work, so I called the agency to ask if

they were sending someone to help me with the kids

for the day. The supervisor told me that the

homemaker called and told them she was knocking

on the door to get in, and no one answered. As I

stated before, I did not go to the appointment, so I

was home, and I know she never came to my house.

I told the supervisor this and asked them to remove

her from the case because she lied. The supervisor

asked me whether she could finish the week out saying that she didn't want to leave me by myself without help for the kids. I said I didn't want her there and we would be fine. The next day she was off the case.

In 2014, my youngest children's father wasn't around. I continued taking care of myself and the kids. At that time, I also decided I wanted to attend law school. I did my research on some colleges and I decided to get my information on NYU law program. I contacted the school to find out more information about its two-year program. After completing the program, I would finish with a master's degree in law. I looked into a class that would prepare me for the LSAT. But my youngest son was starting preschool and he only went for half a day. That would make it a little difficult for me to study. I needed my youngest son to have a full day of school as the at Kaplan LSAT course was only available at 11am. So, I decided to wait to go back to school.

To keep my daughter preoccupied I enrolled her in ballet and Spanish dance classes. Every Saturday, we had to travel to practices. My daughter went to a public school that wasn't doing well, so I started doing work with her at home. I bought a second-grade dictionary and I had her read the words, learn the definitions, and write a sentence using them. We went over math as well. My children will make it in life. My youngest son was in preschool at this time and my older son was in high school. I never want to raise children without giving them a fighting chance.

11. CREATING A LIFE FOR MY KIDS

In the fall of 2015, my daughter was attending second grade in a public school. One day, a woman came up to me and asked me if I knew someone who could watch her daughter for two hours after school. I thought she was a decent woman, so I agreed to pick her daughter up and watch her. I signed the little girl up for dance as well, and I took her with my daughter.

Everything was fine for about two weeks. Then the mother called the school, saying things about my daughter, including that she was bothering *her* daughter. That little girl was bigger than my daughter and older than my daughter. The little girl would never let my smaller daughter do anything to her. The mother called for a meeting at the school with the principal and the parent coordinator. My sister was there as well, and during the meeting both little girls were brought downstairs. The kids apologized to each other and said they were going to be friends again, then they went back to class. The little girl's mother told me, "I know about you, sitting over there." I thought to myself that she was trying to play me, so I told her, "Yes, I am sitting over here... with an education. I'm about to enroll in law school too." Then the little girl's mother got up to fight me—right there in the school office. The principal and the parent coordinator had to get up to stop her from hitting me.

In September of 2015, my son got accepted to a charter school, and that meant my daughter could go there as well. The school setting worked well with what I had going on at home: order, respect, discipline, and hard work.

In April of 2016, I put in a request for a new electric scooter because the electric scooter I had was broken. The insurance denied the request for a new scooter because they didn't feel like they had enough proof from the doctors about why I needed the scooter. My MS doctor sent over a detail description of why I needed electric scooter. Not being able to get around was very disheartening, because I loved accompanying my kids to school in the morning. Sometimes I would also go outside just to get some fresh air, and now that opportunity was also taken away from me. To make things even worse, a new homemaker for my children started. She didn't help me that much. When she came to work, all she did was sleep on my couch and talk on her phone. I took pictures of her doing that and sent it to her agency, so I could report her for not helping me out with my kids. The following week, the agency sent me a new homemaker. She was very helpful and nice. She made sure my kids had dinner and took a bath in a timely matter.

In March of 2017, I spent a week in the hospital. I guess it was due to the stress of too much going on. I had to take my oldest son's father to court over child support, and my younger kids' father was acting crazy. The homemaker's agency called ACS on me, stating that my daughter was having suicidal thoughts. I was just trying to work through everything that was going on at that time, but my body was absorbing all the stress. When I went to the hospital, I couldn't even sit up by myself. I couldn't do anything for myself. I was in the hospital for seven days, and during that time I did two MRIs—one on my brain, and one on my spinal cord. The doctors prescribed me steroids, so I could regain my strength. When I got my results back from the MRI, it showed that the multiple sclerosis was not progressing. When they compared it to the MRI I had in 2012, we could see that the disease hadn't progressed at all since then. I left the hospital with no new chances to my medications and treatment plan. The doctors were looking at me like I was a miracle—they couldn't understand why the disease wasn't progressing.

It's been a year since then, and I still do not have a new scooter. That is a huge problem for me, because that's my only way of getting around. I have learned how to turn a negative situation into positive one. Even though my electric scooter is not working, and I can't take my kids to school or take them to the park, it means I *am* able to stay home and help them with their homework and school projects. That's the best thing I could ask for.

12 MY FEELINGS TOWARD PEOPLE

If I had the opportunity to erase anything that I've had to experience from birth, I would not change anything. Going through these different challenges made me into the woman and mother I am today. I would like to thank everyone who's been in my life for the different experiences they've given me. The past is history, and your future is a mystery. As for being diagnosed with multiple sclerosis, I believe that God would never put more on you than you can bear. My life is not over, it's just beginning. With life, it's mind over matter. I never knew what love was until I had my three children. I didn't know anything, but because of them I was willing to figure out how to truly love. I'm determined never

to raise children who need to recover from a bad
childhood. I gave them all of me because they did
not ask to be here. We went through tough things,
but nothing was enough to ever make me think
about leaving them. I love all three of them equally.

My Dream Me

What I think of as "my dream me" has to do with one of the simplest things in life. A thing maybe that people take for granted. Something that we don't pay any attention to, something that we are least concerned about. Something that we don't worry about, something that we know we will always be able to do—unless something crucial happens. That something is the ability to walk.

One night, I had a dream that I was able to walk again. It was so vivid and so real. I woke up crying. I dream frequently that one day I will get up and be able to play with my children. I dream I will be able to carry them around the house, walk them to the store, and give them a bath. My dream is to be able to run with them in a park, walk up the stairs with them, and sit on the floor while they open their Christmas gifts. My dream is one day I can pick them up without the help of others, prepare them a meal, and take them places that only my oldest son—who is twenty years old—has been.

My dream is being able to do things with my children that other parents are able to do. I am thankful for the assistance that I have, but no one can care for your children the way their own mother can. I want to wake up from this dream and live the life that I once lived. The life that I lived with no regrets. The life that I enjoyed and lived everyday as if it was my last. Before my illness, my dream was to open up a daycare for low-income families in the community. My other dream is to actually find a cure for multiple sclerosis. I dream that I am the first person who finds a cure, and is cured. Not a person who just takes medication and who goes through relapses and remissions.

While other people dream big, and bigger, being able to walk again would be beyond big for me. My dream me is to hold and play with my children.

ACKNOWLEDGMENTS

To my mother and grandmother, I love you guys. I know in my heart you did your best, and I am not mad at you. I love you.

Special thanks to people who have helped me: Tanika Dickenson, Miriam Brown, Shatella Walker, Iris Paul, Precious and Paul Modesto, Jason Boines, Kenyatta Cooks, Hakiem Mack, Curtis Ford, Jamie McBride, Ladawn Fladger, Shaheem Mack, Tiffany Swasey, Dashawna Mack, Signora Waring, Angel Moreira, Santa Delvalle, Jaquan Winters, Alma Mack, and Janny Hernandez. Thank you, guys, for everything.

To my readers, thank you for supporting my book and helping me continue to move my family forward in life. I hope this book has helped you be as strong as you could be. When life comes at you full force, just remember: don't give up.

Made in the USA
Middletown, DE
08 September 2020

18462932R00102